Mystery Mutt

Beverly Lewis

Beverly Lewis Books for Young Readers

PICTURE BOOKS

In Jesse's Shoes • *Just Like Mama*
What Is God Like? • *What Is Heaven Like?*

THE CUL-DE-SAC KIDS

The Double Dabble Surprise
The Chicken Pox Panic
The Crazy Christmas Angel Mystery
No Grown-ups Allowed
Frog Power
The Mystery of Case D. Luc
The Stinky Sneakers Mystery
Pickle Pizza
Mailbox Mania
The Mudhole Mystery
Fiddlesticks
The Crabby Cat Caper
Tarantula Toes
Green Gravy
Backyard Bandit Mystery
Tree House Trouble
The Creepy Sleep-Over
The Great TV Turn-Off
Piggy Party
The Granny Game
Mystery Mutt
Big Bad Beans
The Upside-Down Day
The Midnight Mystery

Katie and Jake and the Haircut Mistake

www.BeverlyLewis.com

THE CUL-DE-SAC KIDS

Mystery Mutt

Beverly Lewis

BETHANY HOUSE PUBLISHERS
MINNEAPOLIS, MINNESOTA 55438

© 2000 by Beverly Lewis

Published by Bethany House Publishers
11400 Hampshire Avenue South
Bloomington, Minnesota 55438
www.bethanyhouse.com

Bethany House Publishers is a division of
Baker Publishing Group, Grand Rapids, MI

Printed in the United States of America by
Bethany Press International, Bloomington, MN

October 2014, 13th printing

ISBN 978-0-7642-2126-2

Library of Congress Cataloging-in-Publication Data
    Lewis, Beverly.
    Mystery Mutt / by Beverly Lewis.
       p.   cm.—(The cul-de-sac kids ; 21)
    Summary: After Jason discovers a homeless dog on his doorstep, he
changes his mind about the Cul-de-sac kids' decision to practice a Fruit of the
Spirit for their new year's resolution.
    ISBN 0-7642-2126-4 (pbk.)
    [1. Fruit of the Spirit—fiction. 2. Christian life—fiction. 3. Dogs—fiction.] I. Title. II. Series: Lewis, Beverly.
PZ7.L58464 Myh   2000
[Fic]—dc21   99-6754

Cover illustration by Paul Turnbaugh
Cover design by the Lookout Design, Inc.
Text illustrations by Janet Huntington

To
Wesley Harris,
who sends me wonderful
letters and likes
reading this series.

THE CUL-DE-SAC KIDS

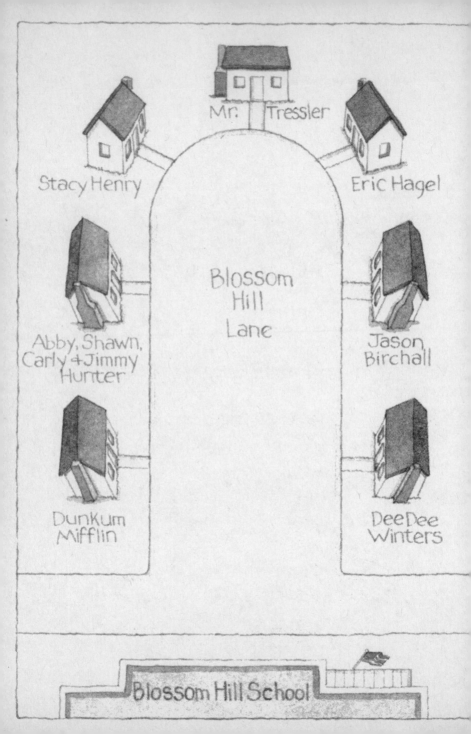

ONE

It was three days before New Year's Eve. Things were popping on Blossom Hill Lane.

Stacy Henry was buzzing with an idea. Her real cool idea had started out teeny-weeny. But during the Cul-de-sac Kids club meeting it grew. And grew.

And grew!

She couldn't keep it to herself any longer.

"Let's do something really fun for the New Year," she suggested.

"Yay!" the girls shouted.

"Like what?" Jason Birchall spoke up.

Stacy twirled her hair. "It's that time of year, isn't it?"

"What're you talking about?" asked Jason, pushing up his glasses. "*What* time of year?"

"I'll give you three guesses, but only three." She squeezed in next to Abby Hunter in the president's seat—a bean-bag chair.

Abby was the president of the Cul-de-sac Kids club. A neighborhood club with nine members. Each club member lived on Blossom Hill Lane, which was really a dead-end street. A cul-de-sac, shaped like a U.

Abby grinned. "I like guessing games. Who wants to guess first?"

"I will!" Dee Dee Winters stood up. She pulled up her knee socks. Then she put her finger on her lip. "My guess is it's time to go group sledding. *That's* really fun!"

Stacy nodded her head. "You're right,

going sledding together is lots of fun. But that's not what I was thinking."

"Who's next?" asked Abby. "This is the second guess, remember."

Dunkum Mitchell raised his hand. "It's time to think about the New Year? Maybe write down some goals or something. That's my guess," he said.

Stacy looked at Abby and whispered, "He's almost got it."

Abby grinned at Dunkum. "Stacy says you're real close. Wanna guess again?"

Dunkum, whose real name was Edward, shook his head no. The kids nicknamed him Dunkum because he was tall. So tall he could dunk a basketball. Every time . . . almost.

"OK," said Stacy. "Since Dunkum nearly guessed it, I'll tell my idea."

The kids leaned forward. Their eyes were big as bowls.

"I want to make some changes in myself," Stacy said. "Like grown-ups do every New Year."

"Oh, no. Not grown-up stuff!" Jason complained. He rolled his eyes and stuck out his tongue. "That's so dumb."

Eric Hagel frowned at Jason. "Don't say 'dumb.' It's not cool. Besides, Stacy's idea might be more fun than you think."

Carly—Abby's little sister—grabbed Dee Dee's hand. They were best friends. "I don't care what Jason says. I wanna make some changes for the New Year, too. Just like Stacy."

"What kinda changes?" sneered Jason.

Stacy said, "Things like asking God to help make me kind and loving. Good changes like that."

Jason clutched his throat when she said "loving."

Yikes! Stacy worried that a full-blown fit was coming.

Quickly, Abby called the meeting to order again. "I like Stacy's idea, too. Keep

talking," she told Stacy.

"Can we name the fruits of the Spirit?" asked Stacy.

Lots of hands went up.

All but Jason's.

Stacy was pretty sure he could say them, too. Jason was just being a pest. But that was normal for him.

"How many fruits of the Spirit are there?" Stacy asked.

"That's easy. Nine!" Dunkum said.

"I almost say that," Shawn Hunter said in broken English.

Shawn was Abby's adopted brother. Their little brother, Jimmy, was nodding, too.

"We know lots of fruit from Bible," Jimmy piped up. "American mother teach us."

Abby's eyes were shining. "Shawn and Jimmy are right. And I think we *all* know the fruits of the Spirit."

"Can we say them?" Stacy asked,

searching for some chalk. "Or maybe we can write them on the chalkboard."

"Good thinking!" replied Abby.

"When we're finished, we'll pick some fruit," Stacy said, smiling. "Each of us can choose a different fruit for the year."

"But we won't eat it," Carly joked.

Dunkum was laughing. "Not unless you want a mouthful of joy or peace."

Dee Dee smirked at Jason. "I think one of us needs the *full-meal deal!*"

Some of the kids snickered.

But Stacy was quiet. She held the board while Abby wrote the nine fruits of the Spirit.

One at a time, the Cul-de-sac Kids called them out:

Love	Goodness
Joy	Faithfulness
Peace	Gentleness
Patience	Self-control
Kindness	

TWO

"I want more patience!" hollered Dee Dee Winters. "And I want it now!"

Stacy chuckled about Dee Dee's choice. It was perfect.

"I pick self-control," Jimmy decided.

Shawn nodded but didn't laugh. "Little brother pick very good fruit," he said. "I pick love—just like Stacy."

Stacy felt her face grow warm. Shawn was looking at her. "Who's next?" she asked.

Carly's hand flew up. "Patience sounds good for me, too." She looked at Dee Dee.

"I wanna match my best friend," she said.

"Joy sounds like a good one," Eric said, his eyes twinkling.

"I think you already have *that* fruit," Stacy said.

The kids agreed.

"Pick something you know you need. Something to improve on," Dunkum suggested.

Eric thought and thought. "OK, I've got it. I'll pick peace. I sure could use some of that." He explained that his grandpa—who lived at his house—was going deaf. "Peace is a good fruit for me to have this year."

Stacy thought Eric's choice was real cool.

Dunkum raised his hand. "I'll pick faithfulness," he said. "Sounds like a good one for me."

Abby spoke up next. "I'll take joy," she said. "And afterward, I want to give it away."

The kids knew exactly what she meant.

"You can't keep joy to yourself," Stacy said.

"That leaves you, Jason," Stacy said. "There's still some fruit to be picked."

"No." Jason shook his head. "I'm not gonna do the fruit thing," he said. "It's silly."

Stacy looked at Abby and shrugged her shoulders. The rest of the Cul-de-sac Kids were quiet.

"OK, that's my idea," Stacy said. "I'm finished."

She turned the meeting back to their president.

But she felt strange toward Jason. Why didn't he want to stick with his friends? What *was* his problem?

THREE

"What's for supper?" Stacy asked her mother.

"Spaghetti and meatballs," Mom said. She pulled out the drawer nearest the table. Knives, forks, and spoons lay neatly inside.

"May I help?" Stacy said.

Mom smiled. "Would you like to set the table?"

"OK!" Stacy always liked helping her mom. She wished she could help even more. Since her dad left, it was just herself and her mom—the two of them. Stacy's mother worked long hours away from home and was often tired in the evening.

"I'll clean up the kitchen for you," Stacy offered. "After we eat."

"That's nice of you." Mom went to check the noodles.

"Is everything under control?" Stacy asked. She watched her mother stir long, skinny noodles.

"They're getting soft. We'll eat soon."

"I love pasta!" Stacy exclaimed.

She meant it, too. Pasta was the best food in the world!

Mom turned to look at her. "That's why I made it. Just for you."

Stacy studied her mom. "You're always so sweet," she said. "Just like the fruit of the Spirit."

"Well, I don't know about that, honey," Mom said. "Nobody's perfect."

"I think you're pretty close," she whispered.

Mom reached over and gave her a big hug. "What's this about the fruit of the Spirit?" Mom asked.

"It's something the Cul-de-sac Kids are doing."

"Really?" Mom seemed pleased.

Stacy felt proud. "It was my idea."

"Tell me more," Mom said.

"You know about making resolutions, right?" she asked. "Especially around the New Year?"

Mom nodded. "Lots of people do this time of year. But not everyone sticks to goals. That's the hard part."

"All my friends have picked a fruit," Stacy explained. "Straight from the Bible."

"And what sort of fruit might that be?" Mom was grinning. She already knew. Stacy was sure of it.

"Things like goodness and love . . . peace and joy." She washed her hands and set the table for two. "I'm picking love," she said.

"What a wonderful choice," Mom said.

"I'm gonna try to love everyone I know. With God's help." She headed for the living room. She wanted to check on her little dog, Sunday Funnies.

She found him curled up near the comics page of the newspaper. "What's with you and the funnies?" she asked. "I always know where to find you, don't I?"

Sunday Funnies barked playfully.

Stacy picked him up. Gently, she carried him into the kitchen. "Time for your supper, puppy dog," she said.

Sunday Funnies made excited sounds.

"Have patience," she told him.

"One of the fruits of the Spirit," Mom added.

"That's right!" Stacy said. "So . . . some patience, please."

She poured dog food into his dish.

Then she stepped aside. "Now have some joy, too," she said.

Mom was laughing.

Sunday Funnies was chowing down.

Stacy was eager for spaghetti!

FOUR

"Good morning, sleepyhead," said Mom. She shook Stacy's shoulder very lightly. "Are you going to sleep all day?"

Stacy stretched and yawned. "It's Christmas break, and I'm still tired."

"OK," Mom said. "I'll let Sunday Funnies out for you."

"Are you leaving for work already?" Stacy asked.

Mom looked at the clock on Stacy's desk. "I'll go in ten minutes," she said.

Stacy sat up. "I guess I slept too late."

"That's all right, honey. You'll be getting up early again soon. Next week when school starts," Mom said with a tender smile.

Stacy swung her legs over the side. "I'm awake now. So I might as well get up."

Mom sat quietly, still smiling.

Stacy yawned again. "I think I'll go visit Jason today."

"How's he doing?" Mom asked.

"Wanna know the truth? He's a pain," Stacy complained.

Mom frowned. "Time to spread some love around. It sounds like Jason Birchall could use a good dose," she remarked.

Usually, Stacy would be thinking: *Icksville!* About showing love to Jason, that is.

Jason was one weird kid. He wasn't easy to love.

Most kids *liked* Jason, though. He was full of fun. And mischief, too.

Even Pinktoes, Jason's pet spider,

liked him. So did Croaker, his bullfrog. Jason wanted to add even more pets to his "zoo."

But love? That was a very difficult subject.

Stacy sighed. She understood her mother. Love was the first fruit of the Spirit. And loving Jason could be tricky at times. But she could do it. God would help her!

"You're right, Mom," she agreed. "I'll go easy on Jason."

"That's my girl," Mom said.

★ ★ ★

Stacy found Jason outside, sweeping snow off his steps.

"Hey, Jason!" she called to him.

He looked up. But when he saw her, he looked back down.

"Are you busy?" she asked, hurrying across the street.

"What's it look like?" he said. He kept

sweeping even though the cement was peeking through.

"I thought we could talk," she said.

"So talk." He glanced over his shoulder at her.

She wondered if she should turn around and go home. Should she even try to show love to Jason?

"Maybe now isn't such a good time," she muttered.

"Maybe not." He kept facing away from her.

"OK. I'll see you later." She headed back across the street. She really thought he might call to her. Tell her to stop walking away and come back.

But he didn't say one word.

Stacy turned to look at Jason from her porch step. She stared at him.

He was still sweeping with his back to her. Jason was doing what he did best. *Being a pain*, she thought.

"It's too bad," she whispered to herself.

"Jason's gonna spoil everything for New Year's."

She opened the front door to her house. With a huff, she went inside.

FIVE

Stacy headed next door to visit her best friend.

"How are we gonna get Jason to pick a fruit?" she asked Abby.

Abby shook her head. "Your guess is as good as mine."

They sat on Abby's bed and lined up the stuffed animals.

"Maybe if we give him some space," said Stacy. "That might help."

Abby's face lit up. "If we give him *enough* space, he might feel left out."

Stacy wasn't sure about that. "I don't

know. That might not be the best way to show love," she said.

"Sometimes loving someone means giving them breathing room." Abby blinked her eyes. "Know what I mean?"

Stacy thought about that. "Maybe."

"So we'll pray," Abby said. "And we'll be patient and gentle with him. Two more fruits."

There was a calendar hanging on Abby's bulletin board.

Stacy counted the days till New Year's. "Phooey," she whispered.

"What's wrong?" asked Abby.

Stacy sat back down on the bed. "We don't have much time."

Abby was nodding her head. "You're right. So we better start praying," she said.

"And we should have another club meeting," Stacy suggested.

"Good idea!" Abby seemed excited about getting together again. "I'll call Dee

Dee and Dunkum. You can tell Eric and Jason. OK?"

Stacy paused. "I . . . I don't know about calling Jason. He might not want to talk to me."

"Why not?"

She told Abby how Jason had treated her this morning. "He could hardly wait for me to leave."

"Are you double dabble sure?" Abby's eyes were big and round.

"I think he's upset about the fruit idea." Stacy hoped she wasn't spreading trouble by talking this way. She wanted to spread love around. God's love.

"I don't know why he'd be upset," Abby said. "Unless . . ."

"Unless what?" Stacy asked. She was eager to know.

Abby leaned back against her pillow. "Sometimes Jason likes to be different. Just to be different. No other reason."

"You're right," Stacy replied. "He gets

more attention that way."

"So we have to *help* him think differently," Abby said.

"That's the hard part," Stacy said.

"He's one stubborn kid," Abby added.

"I guess we *all* are ... sometimes," Stacy agreed.

They listened to CDs in Abby's room for a while.

Soon, Carly knocked on the door.

"Come in," Abby called.

Carly came in, looking surprised. "Don't you want to hear the secret password?" she asked.

Abby looked at Stacy. Her face was red. "I ... I don't know."

"Well, you usually make me say it," said Carly. She shot a look at Stacy. "So ... what're you two doing?"

Stacy almost said "none of your beeswax." But today she was kind. "Just talking," she said.

Abby looked shocked.

"Wanna join us?" Stacy asked Carly.

"Goody!" The little girl jumped up and sat on the bed. "So . . . what're we talking about?" she asked.

Abby smiled. She was going to be kind to her little sister.

Stacy was almost positive.

"We're just talking about Jason and the fruits of the Spirit. We're gonna pray about all that," explained Abby.

Carly's eyes were shining. "I'll help you."

"Good," Stacy said. "The more the merrier."

Carly frowned. "What's that mean?"

Abby told her. "The more people praying, the better."

"About what?" Carly was full of questions. As usual.

Abby's face drooped. She seemed a little angry. But she didn't spout off anything nasty.

Stacy spoke up. "Jason doesn't want to pick a fruit."

"Oh, yeah. I know all about that." Carly grinned. "But I think he'll change his mind."

"That's why we're gonna pray," said Stacy.

"Starting now?" Carly asked.

"Sure," said Stacy.

"Yay!" said Carly.

Stacy and Abby took turns praying out loud. Carly said two sentences and the "Amen" at the end.

"We'll be very kind to Jason," Stacy said. "We promise, right?"

"It's almost New Year's Day," Carly reminded them.

"That's OK. Jason will pick a fruit," Stacy said. "You'll see."

SIX

Stacy's new yo-yo had a rainbow of colors on one side. There was a happy face on the opposite side. The gift had been in her Christmas stocking. It was one of her favorite new toys.

After lunch she played with the yo-yo. And with her cockapoo dog.

"Jason Birchall oughta be bored with his fits," she said.

Sunday Funnies cocked his head. Like he was really listening.

"But you know what?" Stacy continued. "I think something's gonna happen. And real soon."

Sunday Funnies barked, wagging his tail.

"Don't you understand?" she asked. "I mean something wonderful is going to happen to Jason. I just have a feeling."

She looked out the living room window. The street was dusted with clean, fresh snow. Like a frosted cul-de-sac—all fleecy white.

"The world looks white and fluffy, just like you," she whispered. She picked her puppy up and held him close.

"Mm-m, you smell good!" She buried her face in his soft, curly coat. "Did Mom give you a bath yesterday afternoon?"

Sunday Funnies didn't bark yes. But he did bark something. She wasn't exactly sure what he was trying to tell her. Maybe he wanted to go outside.

Yes, that's probably what he wanted.

Stacy waited for her puppy to go out.

She thought of yesterday's club meeting. Mom must've given Sunday Funnies a bath during the meeting.

She decided to take better care of her dog. After all, he was *her* responsibility. In fact, she decided to help around the house more. A lot more!

Soon Sunday Funnies was whining at the door.

She let him inside. "Wanna help me clean house?" she asked.

But he followed the scent of the newspaper. He sat down on the living room floor. Right next to the paper.

"Now, that's a very good way to help," she said. "If you stay out of my way, I'll get the cleaning done much faster."

She went to the hall closet and lugged out the vacuum sweeper. Then she found the plug and turned it on.

Mom will be surprised, she thought.

She could hardly wait to see her mother's face!

★ ★ ★

Minutes later, the doorbell rang.

Stacy didn't really *hear* the bell. But she knew someone was there just the same.

Sunday Funnies had run to the door. He was howling now.

Quickly, she switched off the sweeper. "I'm coming," she called. And she dashed to the door.

There stood Jason Birchall, carrying a cardboard box. "Hi, Stacy," he said.

"Hi." She was very surprised to see him.

"I've got something to show you," he said. He looked down at whatever was in his box.

She stepped back, away from the door. Jason was known to collect strange pets. Things like tarantulas and croaking bull-frogs.

"Uh . . . I don't know," she said. "Maybe not."

"Come on. Just take a look," he said. "This box won't bite."

"But what's inside might, right?" She didn't trust Jason. Not one bit!

He shoved the cardboard box at her. "Surprise!"

"Yikes!" she gasped.

But it wasn't really so bad when she looked inside.

There was no scary, furry spider. Not even a green frog with blinking eyes!

Instead, a shabby little puppy looked up at her from the box.

"Pee-uu-wee," she said, backing away. "Whose dog?"

"That's what *I'd* like to know," he said. "This pooch needs a little kindness. Wanna help me hunt for its owner?"

Stacy was shocked. "What did you just say?"

It sounded like Jason had picked a fruit, after all.

"I asked if you wanted to help me find

the dog's owner?" he repeated.

"That's very *kind* of you," she replied.

He smiled and set the box down. "I knew you'd think so. But don't get any fruity ideas about . . . well, you know."

She knew, all right.

Still, she hoped Jason would change his mind.

Before New Year's Eve!

SEVEN

"Sure, I'll help," Stacy agreed. She stooped down and looked into the box. "The poor thing's shivering."

"And that's not all," Jason said. "He needs a bath, too. And I'm not fooling!"

The closer Stacy's nose got to the homeless dog, the more she agreed with Jason. "Bring him inside a minute," she said. "He could get frostbite out here."

Jason nodded. He lifted the box and heaved it into the entryway. "Someone left him on my front step," he explained.

"You're kidding! They dropped a puppy

off at your house?" Stacy said.

She hated to think of someone being so cruel. She also wondered about the deserted dog. Did it have something to do with her feeling earlier today? That something wonderful was going to happen to Jason?

"I never saw anyone anywhere," Jason explained. He seemed very upset. "Muffie just appeared out of nowhere."

"Muffie? You *named* the dog?" Stacy asked.

Jason pushed up his glasses. "Well, I had to call him something. You can't go around with a poor little dog, calling him nothing. Can you?"

"Yeah, I guess you're right," Stacy replied.

She could hardly believe her ears.

Jason was being very kind! So kind she was sure he'd picked the kindness fruit for the year.

Stacy smiled back at him. "I was just

cleaning house," she told him. She eyed the box. "Better keep Muffie in there till I get my jacket."

Jason stooped down and petted the dog. "Hurry, Stacy, it's getting late. My mom said I couldn't be out long," he urged.

Stacy glanced at the window. The sun was setting fast.

Jason was right. They'd have to hurry.

EIGHT

Stacy rang the doorbell at the first house.

A tall man came to the door. "Hey, kids, what's in the box?" the man asked.

Jason didn't waste any time. "Is this your dog, mister?"

The man shook his head. "Sorry," he said and shut the door. *Slam!*

Just up the street from Blossom Hill Lane, they came to the next house.

"You ring, and I'll talk," Stacy said.

"OK," Jason replied. "But get right to the point. People don't wanna stand at their door on a cold night."

She agreed. Once again, Jason was thinking of others.

When a pretty lady came to the door, Stacy asked the question. "We're looking for this darling puppy's owner." She pointed to the box. "Do you know anything about him?" she asked.

The lady peeked into the box. She said, "AAAGGGHHH!" then slammed the door.

Stacy's teeth were beginning to chatter. "How m-many m-more h-houses?" she asked.

"If you're cold, you should go home," Jason replied. "Muffie's not your problem."

They walked in silence to the next house.

"Do you feel responsible for this dog?" Stacy asked, at last.

Jason shrugged. "I'm not out here freezing my ears off for nothing."

"I know," she said. "I think you're

doing a wonderful thing."

"Well . . . let's not get carried away," Jason shot back.

He rang the doorbell *and* did the talking this time.

The teenager at the door didn't say a word. Just shook his head and closed the door.

"Is this how Mary and Joseph felt on Christmas Eve?" Jason said softly.

Stacy's ears prickled. "What did you say?"

"Nothing," Jason said quickly.

But she was pretty sure she'd heard. *Hallelujah!*

★　★　★

One after another, they knocked on doors or rang doorbells. Nobody but nobody seemed to know anything about Muffie.

"Well, I guess he's ours," Stacy said.

"Ours?" Jason asked. He turned and

looked at her. With a weird look. "What's *that* supposed to mean?"

"Just what I said," she replied.

Then she had another idea. It was the perfect idea! "Maybe Muffie could be our club pet," she suggested. "What do you think of that?"

"I think it stinks," Jason said. "I'm gonna ask my parents if I can keep this mystery mutt."

Mystery mutt? she thought. What a horrible name!

Yet she felt the giggles building up inside her. Stacy held them in. Jason would freak if she let them spill out. He hated giggling worse than almost anything.

"Better give Muffie a bath first," she said. "Your mom won't give him a chance, smelling like this."

Jason nodded. "For once, you're right, Stacy Henry."

"Whatever you say," she answered.

"Can I use your bathtub?" he asked.

"*May* you, don't you mean?" Stacy was picky about speech.

Jason blinked his eyes. "Please, not an English lesson now."

"Hey, do that again," she said.

"Do what again?"

"Blink your eyes like Croaker, your frog," she said.

Then the giggles came.

Jason started running. "Oh, no! I can't stand this," he hollered.

Stacy walked prim and proper to their street, Blossom Hill Lane. All the way, she wondered about Jason. How long before he'd pick a fruit?

She couldn't wait for him to pick, bite, *and* eat the fruit of kindness. Or maybe it would be gentleness!

Whatever it ended up to be, time was running out. The New Year was almost here.

Two days left!

NINE

Stacy and Jason chattered while they scrubbed the mystery mutt.

"Thanks for letting Muffie use your tub," Jason said.

She'd have to clean the bathroom when they were finished. When Muffie was all done with his doggie bath, that is. And . . . before Mom arrived home,

She enjoyed helping Jason. And he seemed to accept her love and kindness.

"Did you hear? We're having another Cul-de-sac Kids club meeting," she said.

"When?" Jason asked. Soapsuds were

all over his glasses and shirt.

"New Year's Eve," Stacy said. She tried not to look at sudsy Jason. But she couldn't help it. He looked so silly.

"What're we gonna do at the meeting?" Jason asked.

She felt the giggles coming. It was impossible to hold them in. "Ha, ha, ha, ha, ha . . ."

"Oh, Stacy, what's so funny?" he said.

"You're all soapy." She pointed to his hair and face.

"I am?" He stood up and looked in the mirror. "Hey, you're right. I *do* look funny. Not only funny, I look like a fruit."

Stacy stopped laughing. "What . . . what did you say?"

"I'm a prune!" He held up his hands. "Look at me."

Jason was right. He *did* look like a fruit.

She stared down at her hands. "Wow, I'm wrinkled, too. Just like a girl prune."

Jason went back to washing Muffie. Stacy helped him dry the dog.

"I guess what's in the heart shows up on the outside," said Jason. "Sooner or later."

Stacy was thrilled. But she didn't dare say a word.

"Count me in—on the fruity loop," said Jason. He was laughing hard. Not giggling, but close.

"What's a fruity loop?" she asked.

"You know what a loop is, right?" said Jason.

"I . . . I guess so." Stacy wasn't really sure.

"A cul-de-sac is sorta like a loop, isn't it?"

Stacy laughed. "Oh, I get it." She said "fruity loop" over and over. "You're one crazy kid," Stacy said.

"Thanks to the mystery mutt, I'm fruity, too!" replied Jason.

"Now we have to convince your parents about Muffie," said Stacy.

"Won't be easy," Jason said. "Even with Muffie smelling nice and fresh, my mom's not much for dogs."

"Maybe *my* mom'll let me keep him," she said.

Just then she heard someone's keys jangle. Stacy looked up. Her mother was standing in the bathroom doorway!

"Oh, hi, Mom," she said. "We needed to give a dog a bath. Hope you don't mind."

"What's going on?" Mom asked, frowning.

"It's a long story," Stacy spoke up quickly.

"Yes, I suppose it is," Mom said. She came into the room and helped dry Muffie.

"Don't worry, I'll clean things up," Stacy promised.

Mom knelt down and petted the puppy. "Whose dog?"

Stacy looked at Jason.

And Jason looked at Stacy.

They both shrugged at the same time.

"We really don't know," Stacy said, at last.

"What do you mean?" Mom asked.

Jason explained everything. "He's a stray."

"How very sad," Mom said about the homeless dog. "But please don't get any ideas, Stacy."

"I didn't think you'd want *two* dogs," Stacy replied.

Jason pushed up his glasses. "Then it's up to me."

Stacy thought he looked awfully happy. Jason *really* wanted Muffie. She was positively sure!

Stacy helped finish drying the dog—with a hair dryer. When he was completely dry, Muffie seemed to smile.

"Look!" Jason said. "Muffie's trying to say 'thank you.'"

"Hey, I think you're right," Stacy said.

She stroked Muffie's white and brown coat.

Sunday Funnies was beginning to whine. He sounded like he was feeling left out.

"Oh, baby," Stacy said, reaching down for her cockapoo. "There's nothing to worry about."

Jason was the one laughing now. "That's right. You're still top dog around here," he teased.

Stacy followed Jason to the front door. "I'll cross my fingers for you," she said.

"Thanks. And say a prayer, too," Jason added.

"I will. I promise," she said.

Stacy could hardly wait to tell Abby!

TEN

"Countdown to midnight!" Stacy shouted.

The Cul-de-sac Kids were trying very hard to have a meeting at Dunkum's. It was turning into a New Year's Eve party.

"Let's see who can stay awake the longest," Dee Dee said.

"That's easy," Carly said. "I'm a night owl."

"So is Jimmy," Jimmy said, pointing to himself.

"Who else wants to stay up to see the New Year?" Abby asked.

"Stacy does," Jason piped up. "Right?"

Stacy wasn't so sure. "Nothing's gonna change, really. There's only one minute difference between today and tomorrow."

Abby jumped out of the beanbag chair. "I think it's time for another change," she said.

"Like what?" said Eric.

"It's time to vote on a new president," Abby said.

"Of the United States?" asked Shawn.

"No, of the Cul-de-sac Kids," Abby replied. "I've been the president all this year."

"That's OK," Stacy said.

"Yeah, we like it this way," Dunkum said. "We voted you in, and you're stuck."

"Till we vote you out," Dee Dee added with a sly grin.

Everyone laughed at that.

Jason stood up, too. "We'll let you know when we're tired of you, Abby Hunter," he joked.

"Thanks a lot," Abby said. Then she sat down again.

"Are you giving up so soon?" Carly teased.

Abby smiled a happy smile. "Just wanted to check and make sure," she said.

Jason kept standing. "I have something to say."

Stacy wondered, *What's this about?*

Why was Jason's face so serious?

Was this about the mystery mutt?

She was nearly holding her breath.

"I acted real stupid at the last meeting," Jason said.

"Not stupid," Dunkum said. "Nobody thinks that about you."

The kids were nodding their heads.

"Just listen," Jason said. He wasn't fooling around. He meant every word. "I picked some fruit this week. Just like the rest of you."

Stacy sighed. This was wonderful. Really wonderful!

Jason kept talking. He wasn't jigging and jiving. He wasn't poking his finger at the air. He was doing his best.

And he wasn't a pain. Not one bit!

"I picked a whole bunch of fruits this week," Jason said.

"You did what?" Dee Dee asked.

Jason was nodding and grinning. "I picked all nine of them. And I'm gonna see how many I can eat this year."

"Yay!" Everyone was clapping.

The girls jumped up and down.

The boys got up and gave each other high fives.

"Jason's real cool," Stacy said. But nobody heard her. There was so much noise.

"This is double dabble good!" Abby shouted.

Finally they sat down again.

All but Jason. He wasn't finished talking. "I wanna thank somebody for all this fruity stuff," he said. He was looking at Stacy.

She ducked her head.

"Stacy's idea was never dumb. The fruity loop is a real cool idea," Jason exclaimed.

"It was God's idea first. Don't forget that," Stacy reminded him.

Carly raised her hand. "I prayed for you, Jason," she said.

"Thanks," he said.

"And you got a new puppy out of the deal," Eric pointed out.

Jason scratched his head. "I can't figure out why my parents let me keep Muffie."

"Because they saw kindness in you," Stacy said.

"And gentleness and joy," added Abby.

"Self-control," said little Jimmy.

"And faithfulness to feed and care for Muffie," said Dunkum.

"Don't forget patience!" Dee Dee and Carly said together.

"Peace, too," said Eric.

"And last, but not least—love," said Stacy.

Shawn was nodding his head. "Stacy's right," he said.

Stacy looked at her watch. "Guess what? It's the New Year!"

"Happy New Year!" Jason was first to say.

Stacy was quite sure that it *would* be happy. Very happy.

With God's help!

THE CUL-DE-SAC KIDS SERIES
Don't Miss #22!
BIG BAD BEANS

Jason Birchall is having bad dreams. Last night three giant carrots chased him to school! His mother's health-food kick is the reason. And he doesn't need the pressure. Jason's trying to earn enough money to buy Eric Hagel's flashy mountain bike. But he's running out of time, and Muffie, his new dog, is no help.

Couldn't ten bucks just drop from heaven?

About the Author

When Beverly Lewis was a little girl, she and her family "adopted" an Eskimo spitz dog. Maxie was frisky and white. He pulled Beverly and her sister, Barbara, on a snow sled to the grocery store one winter. Maxie was also very big and as fluffy as a cloud. When he ran across the yard, his coat seemed to float in midair.

The Fruit of the Spirit part of this book came from Beverly's memories of Vacation Bible School. She and her church friends often had contests to see who could memorize Bible verses first.

Collecting the Cul-de-sac Kids books is lots of fun. Why? Because you don't want to miss a single book!

www.BeverlyLewis.com

*with David Lewis   †4 books in each volume   ‡5 books in each volume